VAMPIRE PETER

For Rebecca – B.M.
For Viago, my favourite vampire – H.P.

First published in Great Britain in 2020 by Andersen Press Ltd.,
20 Vauxhall Bridge Road, London SW1V 2SA.
Text copyright © Ben Manley, 2020.
Illustration copyright © Hannah Peck, 2020.
Romanian translation by Ileana Hunter.
The rights of Ben Manley and Hannah Peck to be
identified as the author and illustrator of this work
have been asserted by them in accordance with the
Copyright, Designs and Patents Act, 1988.
All rights reserved.
Printed and bound in Malaysia.
1 3 5 7 9 10 8 6 4 2
British Library Cataloguing in Publication Data available.
ISBN 978 1 78344 873 9

VAMPIRE PETER

BEN MANLEY   HANNAH PECK

Andersen Press

Peter was the baddest boy in school.
He appeared one day from a faraway land.

And everything he did was strange.

He liked strange things.

And his family were even stranger.

† "Shall I destroy her, your Majesty?"
†† "No, Orlok. She's my friend."

Because Peter didn't fit in,
he didn't have many friends.
And he was always in trouble...

For showing off in gym class.

For scaring Mr Renfield.

For fighting in the playground.

For not telling the truth.

But it wasn't Peter.

It was me.

I opened the cage to stroke Jonathan.
And I forgot to close the door.

I was worried I'd get into trouble, so I said nothing.
And I let Peter take the blame.

After all, he was the
baddest boy in school.

But, when I thought about it,
I knew that wasn't true.

He made me laugh
when I was sad.

He played with me when I
was on my own.

He stood up for me when I was in trouble.

Peter was my friend.

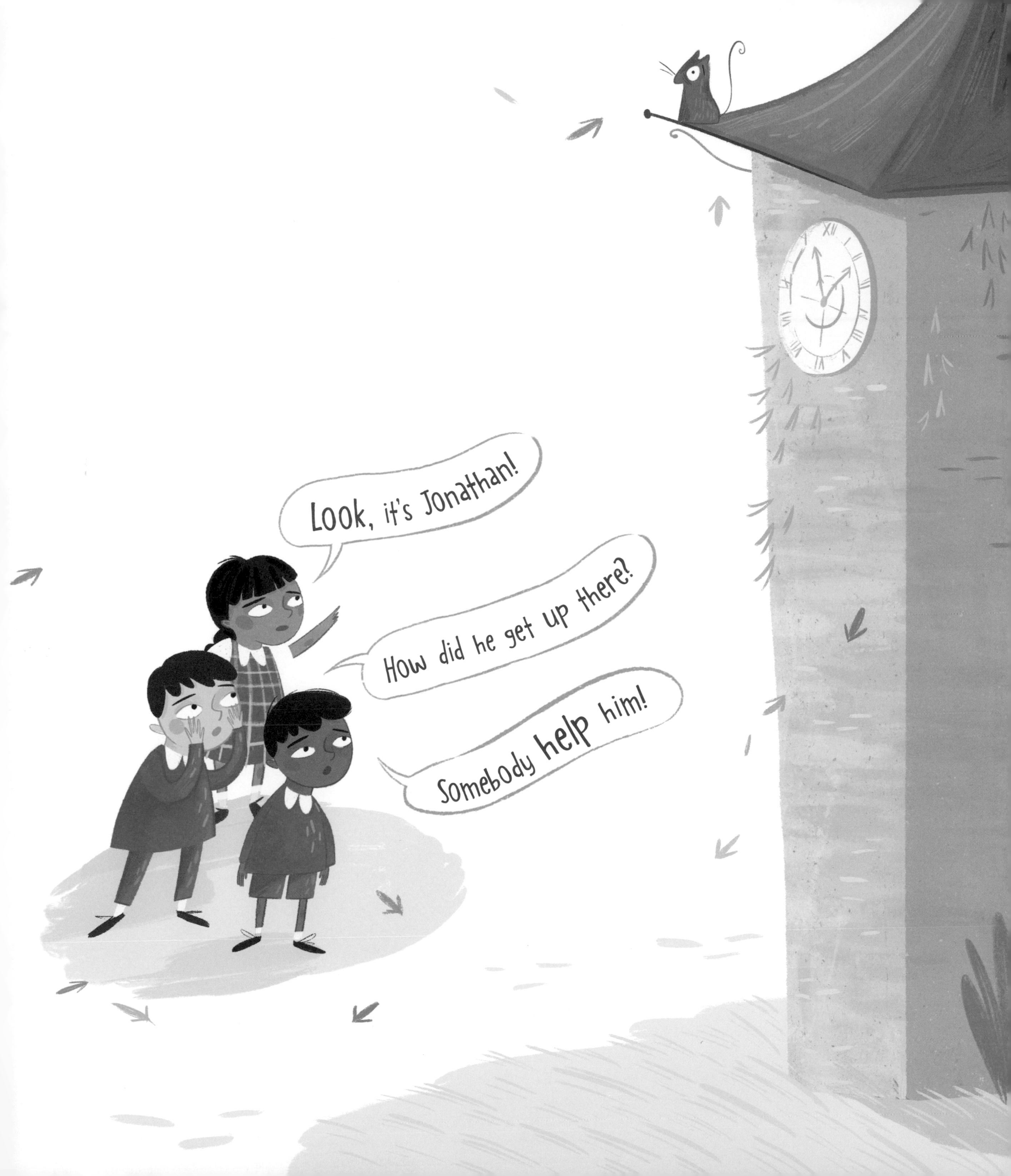
Look, it's Jonathan!
How did he get up there?
Somebody help him!

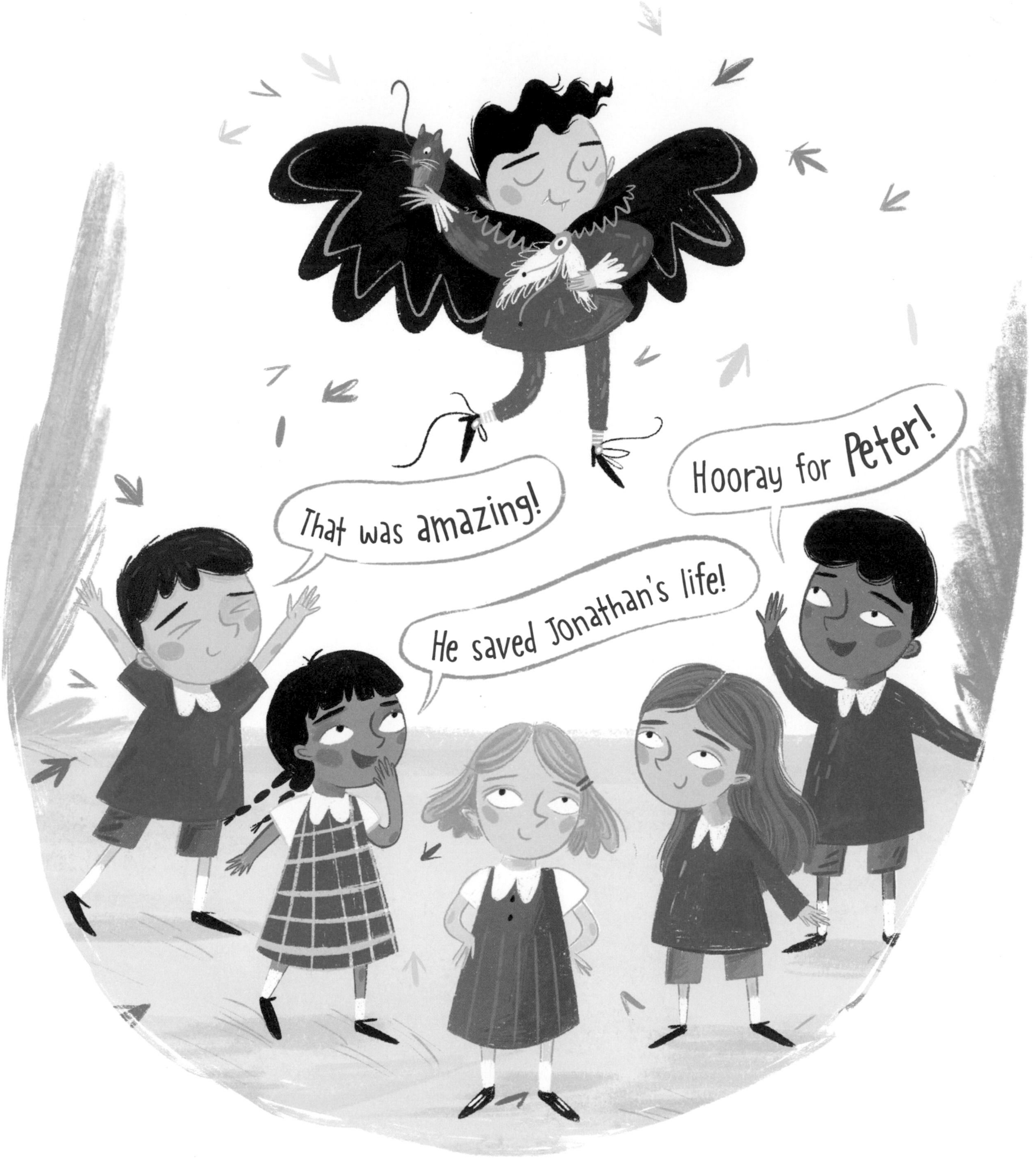
That was amazing!
Hooray for Peter!
He saved Jonathan's life!

I did a terrible thing.
And I thought I would never be forgiven.
But I was wrong.

Everyone said Peter was the
baddest boy in school.
And maybe sometimes he is.

But most of the time,

Peter is the best.